THE Clown-Arounds Go On Vacation

A Parents Magazine
Read Aloud Original.

The Clown-Arounds Go On Vacation

by Joanna Cole
pictures by Jerry Smath

Parents Magazine Press • New York

Library of Congress Cataloging in Publication Data
Cole, Joanna.
The Clown-Arounds go on vacation.
Summary: The Clown-Around family has some
misadventures on its way to visit Uncle Waldo.
[1. Vacations—Fiction] I. Smath, Jerry, ill.
II. Title.
PZ7.C67346C s 1983 [E] 83-13480
ISBN 0-8193-1120-0

Printed in the United States of America.

10 9 8 7 6 5 4 3 2

To Stephanie Calmenson — J.C.

To my aunt, Marie Minch — J.S.

The Clown-Arounds wanted
to take a vacation.
But they could not decide
where to go.

While they were thinking,
a letter came Special Delivery.

It said:

Dear Clown-Arounds,
Please come
to visit me in
my new home.
Just follow
the map →
Love,
Uncle Waldo

MAIL
Why is the alphabet like a mailbox?
They both have a lot of letters.
Clown-Arounds
#9
Funnyville, Ha.
10¢

The Clown-Arounds were excited
about spending their vacation
at Uncle Waldo's.
Mrs. Clown-Around studied the map.

Mr. Clown-Around checked the car.

And Bubbles and Baby
looked at pictures of Uncle Waldo
in the family album.

HOW TO EAT PiE

Then everyone packed a suitcase
and they were ready to go.

FUN
HOW CAN YOU TELL THAT AN ELEPHANT LIKES TO TRAVEL?
HE ALWAYS HAS HIS TRUNK WITH HIM.
CLOWN college

First they stopped to wash the car

and fuel up for the trip.

I SEE AN APPLE FOR "A."
THERE'S A BONE FOR "B."
CAT FOR "C."
H
AB
CD
EFG
HIJK
LMNOP

Then Mr. Clown-Around
looked at the map
to make sure they were
on the right road.
Meanwhile, Bubbles and Baby
played an alphabet game.

When they came to a fork in the road,
they knew it was time for lunch.

So they pulled in at
a fast-food restaurant.

The food was a little too fast,
even for the Clown-Arounds.

Back on the road, Mrs. Clown-Around said, "The map says to turn here for Uncle Waldo's."

But there was roadwork ahead.
So they had to go another way.

Now they were completely lost.
Even the map could not help.

LOOK HOW FRIENDLY THE OCEAN IS.
HOW CAN YOU TELL?
IT WAVES!

They tried going up a winding road.
But that was wrong.

KNOCK, KNOCK.
WHO'S THERE?
RON.
RON WHO?
RON FASTER. THERE'S AN ALLIGATOR CHASING US!

KNOCK, KNOCK.
WHO'S THERE?
LETTUCE.
LETTUCE WHO?
LETTUCE IN. IT'S COLD OUT HERE!
NEWS

They went around a corner.
But that was wrong, too.

They went over a bridge
(oh, no!)...

and through a tunnel.

But they still did not come
to Uncle Waldo's.

The Clown-Arounds were worried.
They were lost
and it was getting dark.

Then Bubbles saw a sign for a hotel.
The Clown-Arounds decided
to stop there for the night
and look for Uncle Waldo's
in the morning.

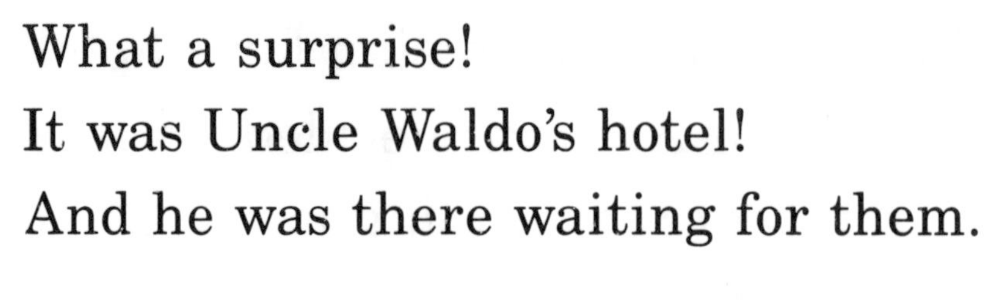
What a surprise!
It was Uncle Waldo's hotel!
And he was there waiting for them.

UNCLE WALDO'S HOTEL
WHEN DO DOGS HAVE EIGHT LEGS?
WHEN THERE ARE TWO DOGS.

The Clown-Arounds think that
visiting family is the best way
to spend a vacation.
Don't you?

MEET MY ANT.
HAVE YOU MET MY ANT?
DOESN'T ANYONE HERE HAVE AN UNCLE?

About the Author

JOANNA COLE, author of the Clown-Around stories, finds herself thinking about these characters often. Recalling her family's most recent car trips she says, "We always seem to make a wrong turn somewhere. Our adventures are never quite as extraordinary as the Clown-Arounds', but we do get where we're going—eventually."

Joanna Cole was an elementary school teacher and a children's book editor before turning to writing full time. She now writes books for and about children and lives in New York City with her husband and daughter.

About the Artist

JERRY SMATH does free-lance illustration for magazines and children's school books. He wrote and illustrated two books for Parents, BUT NO ELEPHANTS and THE HOUSEKEEPER'S DOG. He also drew the pictures for THE CLOWN-AROUNDS, THE CLOWN-AROUNDS HAVE A PARTY and GET WELL, CLOWN-AROUNDS! by Joanna Cole. "It's been a lot of fun bringing the Clown-Arounds to life," says Mr. Smath. "I hope I've done justice to Joanna's lively imagination."

Mr. Smath and his wife, Valerie, a graphic designer, live in Westchester County, New York.